THIS CANDLEWICK BOOK BELONGS TO:

_____

_____

_____

_____

For Jasmine

Text copyright © 1993 by Vivian French
Illustrations copyright © 1993 by John Prater

All rights reserved.

First U.S. paperback edition 1995

Library of Congress Cataloging-in-Publication Data

Prater, John.
Once upon a time / conceived and illustrated by John Prater ;
text by Vivian French.
Summary: A bored boy's world is suddenly populated by three
house-building pigs, a girl wearing a red hood, and other familiar
nursery characters.
ISBN 1-56402-177-7 (hardcover)—ISBN 1-56402-456-3 (paperback)
[1. Characters and characteristics in literature—Fiction.
2. Stories in rhyme.] I. French, Vivian. II. Title.
PZ8.3.P85On 1993   811'.54—dc20 [E]   92-53139

10 9 8 7 6 5 4 3 2 1

Printed in Hong Kong

The pictures in this book were
done in watercolor and crayon.

Candlewick Press
2067 Massachusetts Avenue
Cambridge, Massachusetts 02140

Once
UPON A TIME

Conceived and illustrated by John Prater
Text by Vivian French

CANDLEWICK PRESS
CAMBRIDGE, MASSACHUSETTS

Early in the morning,
Cat and me.
Not much to do.
Not much to see.

Dad's off to work now,
Mom's up too.
Not much to see.
Not much to do.

Day's getting older,
Sun's up high.
Wave to a little girl
Hurrying by.

Mom's cleaning windows.
There's a bear.
He's making a fuss
About a chair.

Ride my tricycle
For a while.
There's an egg
With a happy smile.

Mom's in the garden,
Laundry's dry.
Why do babies
Always cry?

We've got sandwiches—
Cheese today.
Why's that wolf saying,
"Come this way"?

I like jumping
To and fro.
That wolf's howling.
He's hurt his toe.

Mom's drinking coffee
By the door.
I can jump
That far and more!

Sun's going down now
In the sky.
Here's Dad home again!
We say, "Hi!"

Dad's washing dishes.
I look out.
Did I hear someone
Prowling about?

Time for my story.
I yawn and say,
"Nothing much happened
Around here today."

JOHN PRATER, who is said to be "tuned in to the workings of the preschool mind" by *Publishers Weekly,* notes that the most difficult part of illustrating *Once Upon a Time* was working out the "choreography" of the various characters so that they wouldn't get in each other's way. John Prater is also the illustrator of *Little Ghost.*

VIVIAN FRENCH wrote her first poem when she was just four. She is now a master storyteller, enthralling audiences young and old with traditional and original tales. She observes that the boy's "deadpan delivery in *Once Upon a Time* is typical of young children's matter-of-fact attitude toward amazing things." Vivian French is also the author of *Under the Moon, Caterpillar Caterpillar,* an abridged version of Dickens's classic tale *A Christmas Carol,* and a retelling of *Why the Sea Is Salt.*